2009

ATOS Book Level: _____7·16·20__ N|A
AR Points: _____
Quiz #: _____ ☐ RP ☐ LS ☐ VP
Lexile: _____

Here Comes McBroom!

ILLUSTRATED BY

QUENTIN BLAKE

SID FLEISCHMAN

Here Comes McBroom!

THREE MORE TALL TALES

BEECH TREE
New York

McBroom the Rainmaker, *McBroom's Ghost*, and *McBroom's Zoo* first published by Grosset & Dunlap, Inc.

One-volume trilogy, *Here Comes McBroom!*, published by Greenwillow Books in 1992.

Published by Greenwillow Books
a division of William Morrow & Company, Inc.
1350 Avenue of the Americas, New York, NY 10019
www.williammorrow.com

Printed in the United States of America.

The Library of Congress has cataloged the Greenwillow Books edition of
Here Comes McBroom! as follows:
Fleischman, Sid.
Here comes McBroom! / by Sid Fleischman; pictures by Quentin Blake.
p. cm.
Summary: A collection of three previously published stories about the farmer who'd rather sit on a porcupine than tell a lie. Includes "McBroom the Rainmaker," "McBroom's Zoo," and "McBroom's Ghost."
ISBN 0-688-11160-2
1. Children's stories, American.   2. Tall tales—United States.   [1. Tall tales.   2. Humorous stories.]
I. Blake, Quentin, ill.   II. Title.   PZ7.F5992Hd 1992   [Fic]—dc20   91-32689   CIP   AC

First Beech Tree Edition, 1998
ISBN 0-688-16364-5

CONTENTS

MCBROOM THE RAINMAKER

I dislike telling you this, but some folks have no regard for the truth. A stranger claims he was riding a mule past our wonderful one-acre farm and was attacked by woodpeckers.

Well, there's no truth to that. No, indeed! Those

weren't woodpeckers. They were common prairie mosquitoes.

Small ones.

Why, skeeters grow so large out here that everybody uses chicken wire for mosquito netting. But I'm not going to say an unkind word about those zing-zanging, hot-tempered, needle-nosed creatures. They rescued our farm from ruin. That was during the Big Drought we had last year.

Dry? Merciful powers! Our young'uns found some polliwogs and had to teach them to swim. It hadn't rained in so long those tadpoles had never seen water.

That's the sworn truth—certain as my name's Josh McBroom. Why, I'd as soon grab a skunk by the tail as tell a falsehood.

Now, I'd best creep up on the Big Drought the way it crept up on us. I remember we did our spring plowing as usual, and the skeeters hatched out as usual. The bloodsucking rapscallions could be mighty pesky, but we'd learned to distract them. The thirsty critters would drink up *anything* red.

"Will *jill* hester*chester* peter*polly*tim*tom*mary*larry* andlit-

8

tle*clarinda*!" I called out. "I hear the whine of gallinippers. Better put in a patch of beets."

Once the beets were up the skeeters stuck in their long beaks like straws. Didn't they feast, though! They drained out the red juice, the beets turned white, and we harvested them as turnips.

The first sign of a dry spell coming was when our clocks began running slow. We grew our own clocks on the farm.

Vegetable clocks.

Now I'll admit that may be hard to believe, but not if you understand the remarkable nature of our topsoil. Rich? Glory be! Anything would grow in it—lickety-bang. Three or four crops a day until the confounded Big Dry came along.

Of course, we didn't grow clocks with gears and springs and a name on the dial. Came close once, though. I dropped my dollar pocket watch one day, and before I could find it, the thing had put down roots and grown into a three-dollar alarm clock. But it never kept accurate time after that.

It was our young'uns who discovered they could tell time by vegetable. They planted a cucumber seed, and once the vine leaped out of the ground, it traveled along steady as a clock.

"An inch a second," Will said. "Kind of like a second hand."

"Blossoms come out on the minute," Jill said. "Kind of like a minute hand."

They tried other vegetable timepieces, but pole beans had a way of running a mite fast and squash a mite slow.

As I say, those homegrown clocks began running down. I remember my dear wife, Melissa, was boiling three-and-a-half-minute eggs for breakfast. Little Clarinda planted a cucumber seed, and before it grew three blossoms and thirty inches, those eggs were hard-boiled.

"Mercy!" I declared. "Topsoil must be drying out."

But I wasn't worried. Rain would turn up.

What turned up was our neighbor Heck Jones. Rusty nails stuck out of his bulging pockets. He was a tall, scrawny man with eyes shifty as minnows.

"*Hee-haw!*" he laughed. "Drought's a-comin'. You

won't be able to grow weeds. Better buy some of my rain nails."

"Rain nails?" I said.

"Magnetized 'em myself." He grinned. "Secret formula, neighbor. Pound 'em in the ground, and they'll draw rain clouds like flies to a garbage heap."

"Fiddle-faddle," I declared. "Flapdoodle, sir!"

"Why, only five dollars apiece. I'm merely trying to be of service, neighbor. Other farmers'll buy my rain nails—*hee-haw*!" And off he went, cackling through his nose.

Wasn't he an infernal scoundrel, I thought! Setting out to swindle his neighbors into buying rusty old nails at five dollars each!

Well, the days turned drier and drier. No doubt about it—our wonderful topsoil was losing some of its get-up-and-go. Why, it took almost a whole day to raise a crop of corn. The young'uns had planted a plum tree, but all it would grow was prunes. Dogs would fight over a dry bone—for the moisture in it.

"Will*jill*hester*chester*peter*polly*tim*tom*mary*larry*andlittle*clarinda*!" I called. "Keep your eyes peeled for rain."

12

They took turns in the tree house scanning the skies, and one night Chester said, "Pa, what if it doesn't rain by Fourth of July? How'll we shoot off firecrackers?"

"Be patient, my lambs," I said. We used to grow our own firecrackers, too. Don't let me forget to tell you about it. "Why, it's a long spell to Fourth of July."

My, wasn't the next morning a scorcher! The sun came out so hot that our hens laid fried eggs. But no, that wasn't the Big Dry. The young'uns planted watermelons to cool off and beets to keep the mosquitoes away.

"Look!" Polly exclaimed, pointing to the watermelons. "Pa, they're rising off the ground!"

Rising? They began to float in the air like balloons! We could hardly believe our eyes. And gracious me! When we cut those melons open, it turned out they were full of hot air.

"*Hee-haw!*" Heck Jones laughed. There he stood, jingling the rusty nails in his pocket. "Better buy some rain nails. Only ten dollars apiece."

I shot him a scowl. "You've doubled the price, sir."

"True, neighbor. And the weather's double as dry.

13

Big Drought's a-comin'—it's almost here. How many ten-dollar rain nails do you want?"

"Flimflam!" I answered stoutly. "None, sir!"

And off he went, cackling through his nose. Drought wasn't a worry to him. Heck Jones was such a shiftless farmer that he could carry a whole year's harvest in a tin cup. Now he was making himself rich peddling flimflam, flapdoodle, fiddle-faddle rain attractors. Farmers all over the county were hammering those useless, rusty old nails into the ground. They were getting desperate.

Well, I was getting a mite worried myself. Our beets were growing smaller and smaller, and the skeeters were growing larger and larger. Many a time, before dawn, a rapping at the windows would wake us out of a sound sleep. It was those confounded, needle-nosed gallinippers pecking away, demanding breakfast.

Then it came—the Big Dry.

Mercy! Our cow began giving powdered milk. We pumped away on our water pump, but all it brought up was steam. The oldest boys went fishing and caught six dried catfish.

"Not a rain cloud in sight, Pa," Mary called from the tree house.

"Watch out for gallinippers!" Larry shouted as a mosquito made a dive at him. The earth was so parched we couldn't raise a crop of beets, and the varmints were getting downright ornery. Then, as I stood there, I felt my shoes getting tighter and tighter. I looked down. They must have shrunk two sizes!

"Thunderation!" I exclaimed. "Our topsoil's so dry it's gone in reverse. It's *shrinking* things."

Didn't I stay awake most of the night! Our wonderful one-acre farm might shrink to a square foot. And all night long the skeeters rattled the windows and hammered at the door. Big? The *smallest* ones must have weighed three pounds. In the moonlight I saw them chase a yellow-billed cuckoo.

Didn't that make me sit up in a hurry! An idea struck me. Glory be! I'd break that drought.

First thing in the morning I took Will and Chester to town with me and rented three wagons and a birdcage. We drove straight home, and I called everyone together.

"Shovels, my lambs! Heap these wagons full of topsoil!"

The mosquitoes were rising in swarms, growing more temperish by the hour.

I heard a cackling sound and there stood Heck Jones. "*Hee-haw*, neighbor. Clearing out? Giving up? Why, I've got three nails left. Last chance."

"Sir," I said. "Your rusty old nails are a bamboozle and a hornswoggle. I intend to do a bit of rainmaking and break this drought!"

"*Hee-haw!*" he laughed, and ambled off.

Before long we were ready to go. It might be a long-ish trip, so we loaded up with picnic hampers, rolls of chicken wire, and our raincoats.

"Where are we going, Pa?" Jill called from one of the wagons.

"Hunting, my lambs. We're going to track down a rain cloud and wet down this topsoil."

"But how, Pa?" asked Tim.

I lifted the birdcage from under the wagon seat. "Presto," I said, and whipped off the cover. "Look at that lost-looking, scared-looking, long-tailed creature.

Found it hiding from the skeeters under a milk pail this morning. It's a genuine rain crow, my lambs."

"A rain crow?" Mary said. "It doesn't look like a crow at all."

"Correct and exactly," I said, smiling. "It looks like a yellow-billed cuckoo, and that's what it is. But don't folks call 'em rain crows? Why, that bird can smell a downpour coming sixty miles away. Rattles its throat and begins to squawk. All we got to do is follow that squawk."

But you never heard such a quiet bird! We traveled miles and miles across the prairie, this way and the other, and not a rattle out of that rain crow.

The Big Dry had done its mischief everywhere. We didn't see a dog without his tongue dragging, and it took two of them to bark at us once. A farmer told us he hadn't been able to grow anything all year but baked potatoes! We came to a field of sorghum cane and our wagon wheels almost got stuck fast. I thought at first we had run over chewing gum. But no—that sweet cane had melted down to molasses and was dripping across the road.

Day after day we hauled our three loads of topsoil across the prairie, but that rain crow didn't so much as clear its throat.

The young'uns were getting impatient. "Speak up, rain crow," Chester muttered desperately.

"Rattle," Hester pleaded.

"Squawk," said Peter.

"Please," said Mary. "Just a peep would help."

Not a cloud appeared in the sky. I'll confess I was getting a mite discouraged. And the Fourth of July not another two weeks off!

We curled up under chicken wire that night, as usual, and the big skeeters kept banging into it so you could hardly sleep. Rattled like a hailstorm. And suddenly, at daybreak, I rose up laughing.

"Hear that?"

The young'uns crowded around the rain crow. We hadn't been able to hear its voice rattle for the mosquitoes. Now it turned in its cage, gazed off to the northwest, opened its yellow beak, and let out a real, ear-busting rain cry.

"K-*kawk*! K-*kawk*! K-*kawk*!"

"Put on your raincoats, my lambs!" I said, and we rushed to the wagons.

"K-*kawk*! K-*kawk*! K-*kawk*!"

Didn't we raise dust! That bird faced northwest like a dog on point. There was a rain cloud out there, and before long Jill gave a shout.

"I see it!"

And the others chimed in one after the other. "Me, too!"

"K-*kawk*! K-*kawk*! K-*kawk*!"

We headed directly for that lone cloud, the young'uns yelling, the horses snorting, and the bird squawking.

Glory be! The first raindrops spattered as large as quarters. And my, didn't the young'uns frolic in that cloudburst! They lifted their faces and opened their mouths and drank right out of the sky. They splashed about and felt mud between their toes for the first time in ages. We all forgot to put on our raincoats and got wet as fish.

Our dried-up topsoil soaked up raindrops like a sponge. It was a joy to behold! But if we stayed longer, we'd get stuck in the mud.

"Back in the wagons!" I shouted. "Home, my lambs, and not a moment to lose."

Well, home was right where we left it, and so was Heck Jones. He was fixing to give his house a fresh coat of paint—I reckoned with the money he'd got selling rusty nails. He'd even bought himself a skeeter-proof suit of armor and was clanking around in it.

He lifted the steel visor. "Howdy, neighbor. Come back to put your farm up for sale? I'll make you a generous offer. A nickel an acre."

"Preposterous, sir!" I replied, my temper rising.

"Why, farmers all over the county are ready to sell out if this drought doesn't break in twenty-four hours. Five cents an acre—that's my top price, neighbor."

21

"Our farm is not for sale," I declared. "And the drought is about over. I'm going to make rain."

"*Hee-haw*," he cackled. "The Big Drought's only half of it. You don't see any skeeters, do you? But they'll be back, and you'll wish you had a suit of armor, same as me. They chased the blacksmith out of his shop. Yup, and they're busy sharpening their noses on his grindstone. Sell, neighbor, and run for your lives."

"Never, sir," I answered.

But I did rush my dear wife, Melissa, and the young'uns into the house. Then I got a pinch of onion seeds and went from wagon to wagon, sowing a few seeds in each load of moist earth. I didn't want to crowd those onions.

Now, that rich topsoil of ours had been idle a long time; it was rarin' to go. Before I could run back to the house, the greens were up. By the time I could get down my shotgun, the tops had grown four or five feet tall—onions are terribly slow growers. Before I could load my shotgun, the bulbs were finally busting up through the soil.

We stood at the windows watching. Those onion roots were having a great feast. The wagons heaved and creaked as the onions swelled and lifted themselves—they were already the size of pumpkins. But that wasn't near big enough. Soon they were larger'n washtubs and began to shoulder the smaller ones off the wagons.

Suddenly we heard a distant roaring in the air.

Those zing-zanging, hot-tempered, bloodsucking prairie mosquitoes were returning from town with their stingers freshly sharpened. The Big Dry hadn't done their dispositions any good; their tempers were at a boil.

"You going to shoot them down, Pa?" Will asked.

"Too many for that," I answered.

"How big do those onions have to grow?" Chester asked.

"How big are they now?"

"A little smaller'n a cow shed."

"That's big enough." I nodded, lifting the window just enough to poke the shotgun through.

Well, the gallinippers spied the onions—I had planted blood-red onions, you know—and came swarming over our farm. I let go at the bulbs with a double charge of buckshot and slammed the window.

"Handkerchiefs, everyone!" I called out. The odor of fresh-cut onion shot through the air, under the door, and through the cracks. Cry? In no time our handkerchiefs were wet as dishrags.

Well! You never saw such surprised gallinippers.

24

They zing-zanged every which way, most of them backward. And weep? Their eyes began to flow like sprinkling cans. Onion tears! The roof began to leak. Mud puddles formed everywhere. Before long the downpour was equal to any cloudburst I ever saw.

The skeeters kept their distance after that. But they'd been mighty helpful.

With our farm freshly watered we grew tons of great onions—three or four crops a day. Gave them away to farmers all over the county. We broke the Big Drought, and that's how I came to be known as McBroom the Rainmaker.

We didn't hear a hee or a haw out of Heck Jones. Inside his clanking suit of armor he grumbled and growled and finished painting his house. And that was a mistake, for the gallinippers hadn't left the county. They had just flocked off somewhere for a breath of fresh air.

Well, they flocked back. I was standing with my shoes in the earth. My feet had been a torment ever since our dry topsoil had shrunk the leather.

"Little Clarinda," I said. "Kindly plant a vegetable clock. I reckon it'll take one minute exactly to grow these shoes two sizes larger."

She planted a cucumber seed—and that's when the gallinippers returned. Flocks and flocks of them, and my, didn't they look hungry! You could see their ribs standing out. They headed for Heck Jones's house as if he'd rung the dinner bell. That ornery, wily neighbor of ours had painted his house a fool-headed red.

Well! The huge skeeters dropped like hawks. They speared the wood siding with their long, grindstone-sharpened stingers. Must have gone clear through, for we could see Heck Jones in the windows, hammering over the tips.

Oh, he was chuckling and cackling. The gallinippers flapped their wings like caught roosters. Thousands of them! The next thing I knew, all those flapping wings lifted the house a few inches. Then a foot. I was sur-prised to see the floor remain behind—I reckoned

Heck Jones had pulled the nails to sell. Then those prairie mosquitoes gave a mighty heave—and flew off. With the house.

Little Clarinda and I were so dumbfounded we'd forgot about the cucumber clock! It had grown thirty-seven blossoms. I tripped over my own feet, and no wonder! My shoes had grown more'n a yard long.

"K-*kawk*! K-*kawk*! K-*kawk*!"

Glory be! Rain—and it wasn't long in coming. I almost felt sorry for Heck Jones the next day. He could be seen walking his floor without a roof over his head in the downpour.

The young'uns had a splendid Fourth of July. Grew all the fireworks they wanted. They'd dash about with beanshooters, shooting radish seeds into the ground.

You know how fast radishes come up. In our rich top-soil they grew quicker'n the eye. The seeds hardly touched the ground before they took root and swelled up and exploded. They'd go off like strings of fire-crackers.

And mercy, what a racket! At nightfall a scared cat ran up a tree and I went up a ladder to get it down. Reached in the branches and caught it by the tail.

I'd be lying if I didn't admit the truth. It was a skunk.

McBROOM'S GHOST

Ghosts? Mercy, yes—I can tell you a thing or three about ghosts. As sure as my name's Josh McBroom a haunt came lurking about our wonderful one-acre farm.

I don't know when that confounded dry-bones first

moved in with us, but I suspicion it was last winter. An *uncommon* cold winter it was, too, though not so cold that an honest man would tell fibs about it. Still, you had to be careful when you lit a match. The flame would freeze, and you had to wait for a thaw to blow it out.

Some old-timers declared that it was just a middling cold winter out here on the prairie. Nothing for the record books. Still, we did lose our rooster, Sillibub. He jumped on the woodpile, opened his beak to crow the break of day, and the poor thing quick-froze as stiff as glass.

The way I reckoned it, that ghost was whisking about and got icebound on our farm.

The young'uns were the first to discover the pesky creature. A March thaw had come along, and they had gone outside to play. I was bundled up in bed with the laryngitis—hadn't been able to speak above a whisper for three days. I passed the time listening to John Philip Sousa's band on our talking machine. My, those piccolos did sound pretty!

Suddenly the young'uns were back, and they appeared kind of strange in the eyes.

"Pa," said our youngest boy, Larry. "Pa, do roosters ever turn into ghosts?"

I tried to clear my throat. "Never heard of such a thing," I croaked.

"But we just this minute heard old Sillibub *crow*," said our oldest girl, Jill.

"Impossible, my lambs," I whispered, and they went out to frolic in the sun again.

I cranked up the talking machine, and once more Mr. Sousa's band came marching and trilling out of the morning-glory horn. Suddenly the young'uns were back—all eleven of them.

"We heard it again," said Will.

"*Cock-a-doodle-do!*" little Clarinda crowed. "Plain as day, Pa. Out by the woodpile."

I shook my head. "Must be Mr. Sousa's piccolos you're hearing," I said hoarsely, and they went out to play again.

I cranked up the machine, but before I knew it, the young'uns came flocking back in.

"Yes, Pa?" Will said.

33

"Yes, Pa?" Jill said.

"You called, Pa?" Hester said.

I lifted the needle off the record and gazed at them. "Called?" I croaked. Then I laughed hoarsely. "Why, you scamps know I can't raise my voice above a whisper. Aren't you full of mischief today!"

"But we *heard* you, Pa," Chester said.

"Will *jill* hester*chester* peter*polly*tim*tom*mary*larry* and little*clarinda*!" Polly said. "It was your very own voice, Pa. And plain as day."

Well, after that they wouldn't go back out to play. They were certain some scaresome thing was roving about. Sure enough, the next morning we were awakened at dawn by the crowing of a rooster. It *did* sound like old Sillibub. But I said, "Heck Jones must have got himself a rooster. That's what we hear."

"But Heck Jones doesn't keep chickens," my dear wife, Melissa, reminded me. "You know he's raising hogs, Pa. The meanest, wildest hogs I ever saw. I do believe he hopes they'll root up our farm and drive us out."

Heck Jones was our neighbor, and an almighty torment to us. He was tall and scrawny and just as mean and ornery as those Arkansas razorback hogs of his. He'd tried more than once to get our rich one-acre farm for himself.

It wouldn't surprise me if he was making those queer noises himself. Well, if he thought he could scare us off our property, he was mistaken!

By the time I got over the laryngitis, the young'uns

were afraid to leave the house. They just stared out the windows. Something was out there. They were certain of it.

So I bundled up and marched outside to look for Heck Jones's footprints in the mud. Well, I had hardly got as far as the woodpile when a voice came ripping out of the still air.

"Will*jill*hester*chester* peter*polly*tim*tom*mary*larry* andlit-tle*clarinda*!"

That voice sounded *exactly* like my own. I spun about.

36

But there wasn't a soul to be seen.

I don't mind admitting that my hair shot up on end. It knocked my hat off.

There wasn't a footprint to be seen either.

"Do you think the farm is haunted?" Larry asked at supper.

"No," I answered firmly. "Haunts clank chains and moan like the wind and rap at doors."

Just then there came a rap at the door. The young'uns all shot looks at me—Mama, too.

Well, I got up and opened the door, and there was no one there.

That's when I had to admit there was a dry-bones dodging about our property. And mercy, what a sly, prankster creature it was! When that ghost wasn't mimicking old Sillibub, it was mimicking me.

Well, we didn't sleep very well after that. Some nights I didn't sleep at all. I kept a sharp eye out for that haunt, but it never would show itself.

Finally, Mama and the young'uns began to talk about giving up the farm. Then we had another freeze, and for three solid weeks that spirit didn't make a sound. We reckoned it had moved away.

We breathed easier, I can tell you! There was no more talk of leaving the farm. The young'uns passed the time leafing through the mail-order catalog, and we all listened to the talking machine.

"Pa, we'd dearly love to have a dog," Jill said one day.

"You won't find dogs in the mail-order catalog, my lambs," I said.

"We know, Pa," said Chester. "But can't we have a dog? A big, shaggy farm dog?"

I shook my head sadly. A dog would be the ruination of our amazing rich one-acre farm. There was nothing that wouldn't grow in that remarkable soil of ours—and quicker'n scat. I thought back to the summer day little Clarinda had lost a baby tooth. By the time we found it, that tooth had grown so large we had to put up a block and tackle to extract it.

"No," I said. "Dogs dig holes and bury bones. Those bones would grow the size of buried logs. I'm sorry, my lambs."

The icicles began to melt in the spring thaw—and

there came another knock at the door.

The haunt was back!

That night the young'uns slept huddled together all in one bed. Didn't I pace the floor, though! That door-rapping, rooster-crowing, me-mimicking dry-bones would drive us off our farm. Unless I drove it off first.

Early the next morning I trudged through the mud to town. Everyone said that the Widow Witherbee was a ghost seer.

I called on her first thing. She was a spry little cricket of a lady who bought and sold hand-me-down clothes. But tarnation! Her eyesight was failing, and she said she couldn't spy out ghosts anymore.

"What am I to do?" I asked as a litter of mongrel pups nipped at my ankles.

"Simple," the Widow Witherbee said. "Burn a pile of old shoes. Never fails to drive ghosts away."

Well, that sounded like twaddle to me, but I was desperate. She went poking through rags and old clothes, and I bought all the worn-out, hand-me-down shoes she could find.

"You'll also need a dog," she said.

39

My eyebrows shot up. "A dog?"

"Certainly," she said. "Certainly. How are you going to know if you ran off that haunt without a dog? Hounds can see ghosts. Mongrels are best. When their ears stand up and they freeze and point like a bird dog, you know they're staring straight at a ghost. Then you have to burn more shoes."

So I bought one of her flop-eared pups and started back for the farm, carrying a bushel basket of old shoes. As I approached the house, I could see the young'uns' faces at the windows. Piccolos were trilling merrily in the air.

But dash it all! When I opened the door, I saw that no one had a record on the talking machine.

"Confound that haunt!" I exploded. "Now it's imitating John Philip Sousa's entire marching band!"

Of course, the young'uns couldn't believe I had brought home a dog. It was the first time all winter long I saw smiles on their faces. Didn't they gather around him, though! They promised to keep close watch so that he wouldn't bury any bones.

I didn't lose any time burning that bushel of old

shoes. Mercy, what an infernal strong smell! I could
imagine that dry-bones holding its nose and rattling
away, never to return.

Every day after that we walked the pup around the
farm, and never once did he raise his flop ears and
point.

"By ginger!" I exclaimed finally. "The old shoes did it. That haunt is gone!"

By that time the young'uns had decided on a name for the pup. They called him Zip. He grew up to be the handiest farm dog I ever saw.

That rich soil of ours was rarin' to go, and we started our spring planting—raised a crop of tomatoes and two crops of carrots the first day. In no time at all the young'uns taught Zip to dig a furrow. Straight as a beeline, too!

But our troubles weren't over with that ghost chased off. One burning hot morning we planted the farm in corn. The stalks came busting up through the ground, leafing out and dangling with ears. I tell you Heck Jones's hogs acted as if we had rung the dinner bell. Mercy! They came roaring down on us in a snorting, squealing, thundering herd.

"Will*jill*hester*chester* peter*polly*tim*tom*mary*larry* andlittle*clarinda*!" I shouted. "*And* Zip! Run for your lives!"

Those hungry, half-wild razorback hogs broke down the stalks and gorged themselves on sweet ears of corn. Then they rooted up the farm, looking for left-over carrots.

Well, those razorbacks finally trotted home, with their stomachs scraping the ground, and I followed along behind.

"Heck Jones," I said. He was standing in a cloud of flies and eating a shoofly pie. It was mostly made of molasses and brown sugar, which attracted the flies and kept a body busy shooing them off. "Heck Jones, it appears to me you've been starving your hogs."

"Bless my soul, they don't look starved to me." He chuckled, shooing flies off his shoofly pie. "See for yourself, neighbor."

"Heck Jones," I said stoutly. "If you aim to raise hogs, I'd advise you to grow your own hog feed."

"No need for that, neighbor." He laughed. "There's plenty of feed about, and razorbacks can fend for themselves. Of course, if you hanker to give up farming, I might make an offer for that patch of ground you're working."

"Heck Jones," I said for the last time. I could hardly see him from the cloud of flies. "You're mistaken if you think you and your razorbacks can drive us off, sir. Either pen up those hogs or I'll have the law on you!"

"There's no law says I've got to pen my hogs," he said, finishing off the pie and a few flies in the bargain. "Anyway, neighbor, no pen would hold the rascals."

Well, I'll admit he was right about that. We fenced our farm, but those infernal hogs busted through it and scattered the pieces like a cyclone. We strung barbed wire. It only stopped them long enough to

44

scratch their backs. Barbed wire was a *comfort* to those razorbacks.

I tell you we battled those hogs all spring and summer. We planted a crop of prickly pear cactus, but not even that kept the herd out. They ate the pears and picked their teeth with the prickly spines.

All the while Heck Jones stood on the brow of the hill, eating shoofly pies and going, "Hee-*haw*! Hee-*haw*!" His hogs grew fatter and fatter. I tell you we were lucky to save enough garden sass for our own table.

Another growing season like that and we'd be ruined!

Then summer came to an end, and we knew we were in for more than an uncommon cold winter. It was going to be a *dreadful* cold winter. There were signs.

I remember that the boys had gone fishing in late October and brought home a catfish. *That catfish had grown a coat of winter fur.*

That wasn't all. After the first fall of snow the young'uns built a snowman. The next morning it was gone. We found out later that snowman had gone *south* for the winter.

Well, it turned out to be the Winter of the Big Freeze. I don't intend to stray from the facts, but I distinctly remember one day Polly dropped her comb on the floor, and when she picked it up, the teeth were chattering.

As things turned out, that was just a middling cold day in the Winter of the Big Freeze. The temperature kept dropping, and I must admit some downright *unusual* things began to happen.

For one thing smoke took to freezing in the chimney. I had to blast it out with a shotgun three times a day. And we couldn't sit down to a bowl of Mama's hot soup before a crust of ice formed on top. The young'uns used to set the table with a knife, a fork, a spoon—and an ice pick.

Well, the temperature kept dropping, but we didn't complain. At least there was no ghost lurking about, and Heck Jones's hogs stayed home and the young'uns had the dog to play with. I kept cranking the talking machine.

Then the Big Freeze set in. Red barns for miles around turned blue with the cold. There's many an eyewitness to that! One day the temperature fell so low that sunlight froze on the ground.

Now I disbelieved that myself. So I scooped up a chunk in a frying pan and brought it inside. Sure enough, I was able to read to the young'uns that night by the glow of that frozen chunk of winter sun.

Of course, we had our share of wolves about. Many a night, through the windows, we could see great packs of them trying their best to howl. I suspicioned laryngitis. Those wolves couldn't make a sound. It was pitiful.

Well, spring thaw came at last. I remember stepping outside and the first thing I heard was a voice.

"Hee-*haw*!"

"What mischief are you up to now, Heck Jones!" I answered back.

But as I looked about me, I saw there wasn't another soul on the farm.

Then I knew. My hair rose, knocking my hat to the

ground again. That door-rapping, rooster-crowing, me-mimicking, hee-*hawing* ghost was back!

"Zip!" I shouted, and we went tracking all over the farm. Voices popped up behind us and in front of us and around the woodpile.

But that dog of ours never once lifted his flop ears.

"Confound it!" I grumbled to Mama and the young'uns. "Zip can't see ghosts at all!"

The poor mongrel knew I was dreadful disappointed in him. He lit out through my legs and dug a straight furrow in the farm quick as I ever saw. When that didn't bring a smile to my face, he zipped over to the corn bin and took a cob in his mouth. He'd watched us plant many a time. He ran back up the furrow, shelling the corn with his teeth and planting the kernels with a poke of his nose.

"Maybe Zip can't see ghosts," Will said. "But he's a powerful smart farm dog, Pa. Can't we still keep him?"

I didn't have a moment to answer. As the cornstalks shot up, Heck Jones appeared eating a shoofly pie on the rim of the hill. At the same instant his razorback hogs came thundering toward us—and that infernal haunt began trilling like a piccolo.

"Run for your lives!" I shouted.

We all ran but Zip. The corn was ripening fast, and he meant to *harvest* it.

I started back out the door to snatch him up, but suddenly that prankish ghost changed its tune. It began howling like a pack of hungry wolves.

I stood my ground, scratching my head. Sounds were breaking out everywhere in the air. As if howling and yipping like an entire pack of wolves wasn't enough, that haunt joined in with Mr. Sousa's entire marching band. I must admit it had those piccolos down perfect.

You never heard such a howling! And didn't those hogs stop in their tracks! I tell you they near jumped out of their skins. That ghost kept yipping and howling from every quarter. Heck Jones didn't have a chance to *hee* and to *haw*. Those razorbacks turned on their heels. They trampled him in the mud and kept running—though one of them did come back for the shoofly pie. My, they did run! I heard later they didn't stop until they arrived back in Arkansas, where they were mistaken for guinea pigs. They had run off that much weight.

"Yes, my lambs," I said to the young'uns. "Reckon we'll keep ol' Zip. Look at him harvest that corn!"

Well, we'd got rid of Heck Jones's razorback hogs, but we still had that dry-bones cutting up. The young'uns remembered to be scared and streaked behind closed doors.

I kept scratching my head, and suddenly I said to myself, "Why, there's no haunt around here. No wonder ol' Zip couldn't spy it out."

Glory be! It was clear to me now. There never *had* been a haunt lurking about! It was nothing but the weather playing pranks on us. No wonder we hadn't been able to hear wolves in the dead of winter. *The sounds had frozen.*

And now all those sounds were *thawing* out!

Well, it wasn't long before I coaxed the young'uns outside again, and soon they were enjoying the rappings at the door and the yips of wolves and shotgun blasts three times a day from the chimney top.

And didn't they laugh about Heck Jones's razorback hogs running from the howling and yipping of last winter's wolves!

Well, that's the truth about our prairie winters and McBroom's ghost—as sure as I'm a truthful man.

McBROOM'S ZOO

Beasts and birds? Oh, I've heard some whoppers about the strange critters out here on the prairie. Why, just the other day a fellow told me he'd once owned a talking rattlesnake. It didn't *talk*, exactly. He said it shook its rattles in Morse code.

Well, there's not an ounce of fact in that. Gracious, no! That fellow had no regard for the truth. Everyone knows that a snake can't spell.

But yes, we did collect some mighty peculiar and surprising animals here on our wonderful one-acre farm. It's not generally known that we had the only Great Hidebehind in captivity. I must not forget to tell you about it.

If you've heard of me—Josh McBroom—you know that I'm a stickler for the honest facts. Why, I'd rather sit on a porcupine than tell a fib.

Of course, there are beasts and birds that come and go with the weather, so I'd best start with that ill-tempered spring morning. A low, ashy-looking cloud stretched from one horizon to the other, and the air was quiet. *Uncommonly* quiet. Not a note of birdsong to be heard. But I paid it no mind, and we planted our farm in tomatoes.

I reckon you know about that astonishing rich top-soil of ours. My, it was a wonder! There was nothing you couldn't grow on our farm and quicker'n lickety-whoop. Why, just last Wednesday one of the young'uns left a hand trowel stuck in the ground and by morning it had grown into a shovel.

But to get back to those tomatoes. It wasn't five minutes before the vines were winding up the wood stakes and putting out yellow blossoms. Soon our one-acre farm was weighted down with green tomatoes. As they swelled up and reddened, we had to work fast before the stakes took root.

"Will*jill* hester*chester* peter*polly*tim*tom*mary*larry* andlittle*clarinda*!" I called to the young'uns. "Time to harvest the crop. Looks like thirty tons, at least!"

"And look what's coming, Pa!" little Clarinda shouted.

She pointed off toward the northwest, and I about jumped out of my shoes. There appeared to be a stout black rope dangling from the clouds in the distance. "Tornado!" I yelled. "Into the storm cellar, my lambs! Run!"

The young'uns' dog, Zip, began to yip. We streaked it to the house, where my dear wife, Melissa, was taking a rhubarb pie out of the oven.

"Twister coming, Mama!" Polly cried out.

"And heading this way!" Will added, glancing out the window.

We all tumbled down into the storm cellar and shut the slanting doors after us. We could hear a whistling in the air as that twister drew closer. There was nothing to do now but wait it out in the darkness underground.

"Do you think it'll carry off the house?" Jill asked.

"And your Franklin automobile, Pa?" asked Chester.

"Why, our farm's too trifling small for a whirlwind to go out of its way for," I said. "Nothing to worry about, my lambs."

But the whistling in the air became a screech, and we knew that cyclone wasn't far off. The screech became a howl, and we knew it was closer still. The howl became a roar, and we knew that infernal twister was upon us!

The young'uns covered their ears. Mercy! The very earth shook. Overhead we could hear the house windows explode. And for a last moment it seemed that all the air in the cellar was sucked up and away. At least I believe that's what made our hair shoot up on end.

Then the roar faded to a howl, and the howl to a screech, and the screech to a whistle. I was dead certain our house had gone up in sticks and the air-cooled Franklin automobile with it. I scampered up into the daylight.

"Glory be!" I shouted. "Come see for yourselves!"

The house was still standing. And the Franklin, too!

But our joy hardly lasted a moment. That infernal freak of nature had come so close it had plucked our entire crop of ripe red tomatoes—vines, stakes, and all.

Worse than that—*it had sucked up our powerful rich topsoil*. Every glorious handful! We found ourselves gazing at a one-acre hole in the ground where our farm had been. You'd think that tricky twister had paused a moment to scoop it out clean.

"Oh, Pa." My dear wife, Melissa, began to cry, and the young'uns joined in.

I set my jaws and strode toward the old Franklin. "Dry your tears, my loves," I said. "That whirlwind is bound to tucker itself out and drop our farm somewhere. I aim to race after it."

Well, the Franklin was still standing, but in no condition to race. Tarnation! That pesky tornado had sucked the air out of the tires.

"Will, fetch the tire pump," I said. "Not a moment to lose!"

The boys and I took turns pumping up the tires. We had hardly got started when Zip sniffed out something alive cowering under the car. Peter crawled underneath and dragged the creature out.

No. It wasn't the Great Prairie Hidebehind.

But it was a mighty odd beast—never saw anything like it before. It appeared to be a small mountain goat with the tail and ears of a large white-tailed jackrabbit—but that wasn't what made it odd. No, indeed, the surprising thing was its legs. The beast wasn't constructed to stand on level ground. The legs on one side were amazing short and the legs on the other side were amazing long. The poor creature was a bit dazed; it must have fallen out of the tornado along the way.

We had got the last tire pumped up when the girls gave a shout. Polly had run into the house to find the natural history book and turned up a picture of that wrong-legged beast. "Pa, it's a Sidehill Gouger!" she said.

Oh, it was mighty rare, the book said. It lived on steep hillsides and needed those two long legs and two short legs to walk upright. Of course, it went around

and around one way only; it would tumble over if it tried to go the other.

"Can we keep it, Pa?" the girls asked, one after the other.

"We don't have any steep hillsides around here," I reminded them, and jumped into the Franklin. Will and Chester jumped in, too. They wanted to go chasing after that cyclone with me.

Well, it wasn't hard to follow. Gracious, no! It had not only snatched up our tomatoes but emptied a bin of onions and sucked up three barrels of cider vinegar

I had set out to age. You could see that twister for miles, spinning away as red as ketchup.

In fact, it *was* ketchup. As we raced along we could see it squirting everything in its path—barns, windmills, and a bald-headed fellow tacking up KEEP OUT signs who hadn't dodged out of the way fast enough. He said later it was the best tomato ketchup he had ever tasted, though it was a mite gritty. But he didn't mind that. Our topsoil in that ketchup tornado had grown hair on his head.

Well, we must have chased that whirlwind forty miles across the prairie. About the last thing it found to rip up was a stretch of barbed wire. Then it ran out of mischief, so to speak. It dropped our farm in a great red heap and wasted away to the small end of nothing.

When we reached our pile of topsoil, we could hardly believe our eyes. That freak of nature had not only fenced it with tomato stakes and barbed wire—it had even tacked up the KEEP OUT signs.

"Pa, how'll we ever fetch it all home?" Chester asked.

I scratched my head. It looked like two hundred wagonloads, at least, sitting on someone else's land.

We'd be lucky if they didn't charge storage. My, what a heap of money it would cost to haul that farm forty miles back where it came from!

"Boys," I said softly. "Might as well head back home. Looks like we're tornadoed out of business. Unless we can figure some way to raise a mighty sum of money."

Just then Will pricked up his ears. "Hear that, Pa? Sounds like a tin teakettle steaming away."

"There are no teakettles out here," I said.

"I hear it, too," Chester said. "And *there* it is!"

Well, it wasn't a tin teakettle. It was a peculiar-looking bird wailing away inside the barbed wire fence. *Mighty* peculiar. For one thing, it wore its feet backward.

No. It wasn't the Great Hairy Prairie Hidebehind.

The boys crawled through the barbed wire and fetched the sad creature. It was about the size of a small turkey, only larger, and the cyclone had plucked all its feathers. The most surprising feature was its beak. It was shaped like the spout of a teakettle, and every time the bird made that teakettle-boiling sound, why, steam came pouring out.

I shook my head in amazement. "I declare if that twister hasn't flushed some mighty uncommon livestock out of hiding," I said.

"Can we take it home?" the boys asked.

I shook my head and cranked the Franklin. "With all its feathers gone the poor thing's bound to expire."

Well, the boys packed that nameless bird in ketchupy topsoil mud, and before we had driven three miles, a new crop of feathers began to sprout! They were the color of green tea, except the tail feathers. Those were sterling silver and shaped like teaspoons.

All the way back we saw dazed chickens and pigs and prairie dogs caught up by that howling twister and spun away far from home. But the boys had lost interest in common barnyard animals. They now fancied themselves rare game collectors.

We couldn't have been more than a mile from home when Will shouted, "There's something, Pa!"

The boys jumped out and started chasing a catfish through the dust.

Well, there's nothing uncommon about a cat-fish—but this one appeared to be swimming through the dust *backward*. Making good time, too. Gave the boys a merry chase!

They did manage to corral the confused fish. They flopped him in the backseat, and we rushed on home to get him in a tub of water before it was too late. I reckoned the twister had whirlwinded him out of a creek somewhere.

But I was dead wrong. That ungrateful rascal leaped right out of the water back into the dust. It had a considerable *dislike* for water.

Turned out the boys had caught a genuine Desert Vamooser—very rare. It swims tail first to keep the dust out of its eyes.

And wasn't I surprised to see how that wrong-legged Sidehill Gouger had made himself right at home! There he was, running counterclockwise around the sides of our one-acre hole in the ground, happy as a squirrel and pausing only to gouge out shallow and mysterious pockets.

The young'uns turned the Desert Vamooser loose in the bottom, and I gathered the family together to break the bad news about our topsoil.

"Maybe another twister will come along and fetch it back," Polly said hopefully.

That wasn't likely, and Mama began dabbing at her eyes with her apron. "I must have left the teakettle boiling," she remarked suddenly.

Mercy! We had forgot that shy, spout-nosed, vapor-blowing creature in the back of the car, and it had got lonely. The young'uns crowded around and gazed at it in wonder.

"Look, Pa, its feet point behind it," Larry said.

Well, it didn't take long to discover what nature of

bird the boys had found. It was a Silver-Tailed Teakettler—very rare. The book said no hunter had ever
tracked one down to pluck its wonderful sterling silver
tail feathers.

And little wonder! I reckoned we knew something
that wasn't in the book—those wrong-way feet. We let
it out and saw that it left backward footprints. My, that
was clever! Anyone following those tracks would pro-
ceed where the Teakettler had *been,* not where it was
going.

"Pa," little Clarinda blurted out. "We've got us a zoo.
Our very own zoo! We could charge a penny."

"A nickel," Larry declared.

"A dime," Mary said.

"A quarter, at least," Tim insisted. "Didn't Pa say it
will take a heap of cash money to fetch back the
farm?"

A zoo! The thought near took my breath away.
Wouldn't folks come from miles around to see these
rare creatures? It wouldn't surprise me if we had the
only Teakettler, Desert Vamooser, and Sidehill Gouger
in captivity.

"Glory be!" I exclaimed. "A zoo, did you say? Why, a zoo we'll have! No telling what other rare beasts that twister twisted up and scattered along the way. Not a moment to lose, my lambs!"

Well, the young'uns scurried after butterfly nets and gunnysacks to go collecting—all except Will. "Pa," he called, stooping at the rear of the Franklin. "Look at these tracks—coming all the way down the road. Far as the eye can see. I do believe something followed us home."

My, but they were outlandish paw prints! Clearly a two-legged beast that appeared to walk only on the tips of its toes. Toes? Why, it had *seventeen* toes—eight on the left foot, nine on the right.

"We must have scared it off," I remarked, looking all about. And when the young'uns turned up ready to set out, I said, "Keep your eyes peeled for a seventeen-toed critter. That would be a fine catch for our zoo."

Well, the whole family spread out along the twisty path of the tornado. By early candlelight we returned home with several uncommon beasts and birds, including a rare Spotted Compass Cat—its tail always pointed north. But we'd seen neither hide nor hair of that two-legged, seventeen-toed visitor.

What we did see—standing at the very edge of our one-acre hole in the ground—was a two-legged, hairy-faced varmint that I recognized to be a man. He had a shotgun in one hand, a deer rifle in the other, a revolver in his belt, and a large skinning knife between his teeth.

He was raising the rifle to his shoulder when I gave a shout. "What in tarnation do you think you're doing, sir! Who are you?"

The rifle exploded. "Tarnation yourself!" he shouted. That man could talk with the skinning knife between his teeth. "You made me miss! I want that Sidehill Gouger and mean to have him—stuffed and mounted. I'm a hunting man, that's who I am, and I've got a hunting license to prove it."

I was bristling mad. "Well, you're trespassing, and you don't have a license for that. Furthermore and what's more, this is a zoo, sir, and you can't hunt in a zoo."

"A *zoo*!" He laughed. That man could even laugh with the skinning knife between his teeth. "I don't see any signs. Light's failing. I'll be back."

Of course, I stood guard all night long. The young'uns busied themselves making signs and we posted them all around our farm.

MCBROOM'S ZOO

NO HUNTING ALLOWED!

Well, that fellow didn't show up at the crack of dawn. But a flock of sage hens did. They made nests in the hillside gouges the Sidehill Gouger had gouged out. I declare, those hens had been searching for him! It turned out they weren't true sage hens. They

were Galoopus Birds—very rare. Nesting in the steepest places, the Galoopus laid square eggs so they couldn't roll off down the slopes.

As the morning brightened, I noticed there were more of those tiptoe tracks about—and very fresh.

"Jill," I said. "Is there anything in the natural history book about a seventeen-toed animal?"

She went to look it up while the other young'uns scampered off to post signs announcing the opening of our zoo. That flock of Galoopus Birds would be a fine addition, not to mention the critters we had brought back in gunnysacks the day before. The prize of the lot was a toothy, moose-headed Spitback Giascutus, and it did come in handy.

For just then that two-legged, hairy-faced man turned up. I did wonder if he had seventeen toes, but he was wearing boots.

"You can see the signs," I snapped.

"Oh, I can see the signs." He chuckled between the skinning knife in his teeth. "But I can't read."

Quick as lightning he raised the rifle and fired. I thought sure he had bagged our Sidehill Gouger, but no, he had taken a sudden fancy to the moose-headed Giascutus. And that was a mistake. No one had *ever* been able to shoot a Spitback Giascutus.

What happened next was truly amazing! The Giascutus raised its antlers and caught the lead ball between its teeth. He spit it right back with remarkable aim and took a nick out of that infernal hunter's left ear.

Didn't he leave in a hurry, though! He'd never been shot at by an animal before. But I feared he'd be back.

Jill came hurrying out of the house with the book. "Pa, the only seventeen-toed creature known is the Great Seventeen-Toed Hairy Prairie Hidebehind—and it's extinct."

"Extinct?" I replied thoughtfully. "Well, it may be extinct in the book, but there's one alive and lurking around here somewhere. And I declare if those don't look like fresh tracks just behind you."

I didn't mean to scare her—but she did jump back. Not that there was a creature to be seen. According to the book, no one had *ever* laid eyes on a Hidebehind. It was always hiding behind something. Oh, it was slick at the game. A Hidebehind could be following you on its tiptoes, but it did no good to look. Every time you spun around it would still be hiding behind you!

Well, the news spread quickly that we had a dry-land fish that swam backward and birds that laid square eggs. A few folks turned up, and then more folks and

before long whole crowds of folks—some from out of state! The young'uns charged a quarter—kids free—and took turns lecturing on the surprising habits of our animals.

My, didn't we do a brisk business! Mama made barrels of lemonade, and I slept in the daytime so I could stand watch at night. That hunter with all his guns was a worry. And I did mean to have a look at the Great Seventeen-Toed Hairy Prairie Hidebehind.

I tell you, it was a mite scary guarding the zoo at night. I was certain that Hidebehind was following me about, but every time I whirled around it whirled around, too. I even tried walking about with a hand mirror, but the Hidebehind was too eternal clever for tricks like that.

But one night, when I whirled around, I saw that ornery hunter sneaking down among the zoo animals. He barely got his rifle raised before the Teakettler steamed out a warning. The Desert Vamooser streaked backward and threw a large fishtail full of dust into his eyes. Ruined his aim, of course—near blinded him for a month, it seemed.

By that time we had raised enough cash money to tote back our topsoil. Everyone agreed we had best turn the uncommon creatures back into the wild where they belonged. Of course, the young'uns hated to part with them. And I do believe the animals were happy with us. But there was the danger they would end up, one by one, on that two-legged varmint's wall—stuffed and mounted.

So the next morning we took down the zoo signs and loaded up the car with animals—mercy, there was hardly room for the young'uns!—and took off for the wildest parts of the prairie. We found a dusty old riverbed for the Desert Vamooser, but it fell dark before we discovered a sidehill for the Sidehill Gouger. We didn't rightly know what sort of country the Silver-Tailed Teakettler came from, but it began to steam happily as we ran through a patch of poison ivy, and we dropped it off there.

Well, you might think we'd get lost chasing about in the middle of the night in the middle of nowhere, but far from it. Didn't we have that Compass Cat with its tail always pointing due north? It was the last animal we turned loose.

Our farm? Oh, we got the topsoil hauled back—the wagons stretched out for half a mile, and it took the better part of a week. But my thoughts were still on that Great Seventeen-Toed Hairy Prairie Hidebehind.

Every morning I found fresh tracks. I *did* want to have a look at it. I began practicing whirling about—faster and faster.

Well, I got mighty fast. Before breakfast one morning I was out by the well and felt certain I was being followed. I whirled about quick as you please—and saw that backward-footed Silver-Tailed Teakettler. It had come back.

"Will *jill* hester*chester* peter*polly*tim*tom*mary*larry* andlittle*clarinda!*" I called, and they came bounding outside. "Looks like that fellow means to stay. You've got a new pet."

Well, they took the Teakettler inside the house—and just in time. Not a moment later that hairy-faced hunting man turned up armed to the teeth, as usual, and wearing goggles. He didn't mean to have dust thrown in his eyes again.

"You're too late," I said. "The animals are gone—every one."

"I see fresh tracks," he answered gleefully, lowering his nose to the ground like a bloodhound. "Reckon I'll follow them and bag myself that big bird."

He couldn't see too well with those goggles on. He overlooked the Hidebehind's paw prints and went loping away, following the Teakettler's backward tracks. As far as I know, he followed them right back where they started—a hundred miles across the prairie in a patch of poison ivy. We never saw him again.

But I did see the Great Seventeen-Toed Hairy Prairie Hidebehind! Indeed, I did! Not that I ever learned to whirl about fast enough—without help.

It was dusk, and I sat down on a small wood stump to shake a rock out of my shoe. Only it wasn't a small wood stump. It was a porcupine with its quills up! Didn't I jump! And didn't I whirl about *quick*!

Glory be! There he stood—the Great Seventeen-Toed Hairy Prairie Hidebehind!

Well, that shy beast was so embarrassed to be seen that he immediately hid behind *himself*. At least, I reckon that's what happened, for he just seemed to spin out of sight. A few tufts of orange hair settled to the earth like feathers.

We never saw his tracks around our wonderful one-acre farm again. But I'm certain he's still lurking about somewhere, hiding behind someone. Of course, he's quite harmless.

Mercy! He could be hiding behind YOU.

SID FLEISCHMAN was awarded the 1987 Newbery Medal for *The Whipping Boy*. He was born in Brooklyn and grew up in San Diego. He worked as a professional magician and newspaperman before turning to fiction writing. He is a master of the comic novel, and his books have been translated into sixteen languages. A number of them have also been made into motion pictures.

His popular books include *The Whipping Boy, Jim Ugly, The Midnight Horse, The Ghost in the Noonday Sun, Mr. Mysterious & Company, Chancy and the Grand Rascal, Humbug Mountain, The Scarebird,* and *The Hey Hey Man.*

The father of three children (one of whom is the writer Paul Fleischman), he lives in Santa Monica, California.

QUENTIN BLAKE was born in London and attended Downing College, Cambridge. His cartoons and illustrations have appeared in *Punch, The Spectator,* and many other magazines. He began illustrating children's books in 1960. He is the author-artist of *Quentin Blake's ABC* and *All Join In,* among many other distingiushed books, and the illustrator of many of the stories of Roald Dahl as well as books by Joan Aiken and Russell Hoban. He lives in England.